The Ugly D

retold by Carrie Smith
illustrated by Jacqueline Rogers

Make Connections

Which of these animals have you seen before? Where and when did you see them?

A duck sat on her eggs.
She sat for a long time.
Then one day some ducklings
came out of the eggs.

Five ducklings were little.
One duckling was big and gray.
"You are ugly," said the
little ducklings.

The big duckling got bigger.
He got uglier, too. The ducks
were not nice to the ugly duckling.
"You are ugly," they said.

The ugly duckling was sad.
He was very, very sad.

The ugly duckling went away.
He was all alone.

One day, the ugly duckling saw some ducks.
They said, "Oh, you are so ugly!"
Then the ducks went away.

The days got cold. The leaves fell.

The days got colder.
The snow fell. The duckling
was cold. He was all alone, too.

After a long time, the snow went away. The trees were green. The ugly duckling was very big now.

He looked into the water.
He saw a beautiful bird.
"Look at that bird," he said.

Then the ugly duckling saw
some other birds. They looked like
the bird in the water.
The ugly duckling asked,
"Who are you?"

"We are swans like you," they said.

"But you are so beautiful," said
the ugly duckling.

"So are you," said the birds. "Look!"

Then the ugly duckling was not sad. He was very happy. He was a beautiful swan!